Praise for Other Work

"What a fun, witchy little read! The Horned Women takes a creepy old Irish fairy tale and spins it into something fresh, smart, and totally charming. I loved Maura — she's got that "holding it together with duct tape and coffee" energy I can seriously relate to — and seeing her face off against twelve different horned witches with nothing but folklore, stitching skills, and pure mom grit was just so satisfying.

Christy Matheson writes with a cozy, heartfelt vibe that makes even the spookiest moments feel grounded and real. It's a quick read, but it really sticks with you. If you like your fairy tales with a bit of chaos, a little magic, and a lot of heart, you'll love this one."

—Gina Rae Mitchell Reviews

"Christy Matheson takes ancient folklore and breathes wild, bloody life into it, conjuring up a story of grief, anger, magic, and survival.

The atmosphere is thick with shadow and myth: dark woods, whispered warnings, the gleam of horns; I was spellbound. The characters are raw, fierce, and painfully real. Maura is a woman who refuses to be quiet and refuses to be broken. She may not be unscathed but she has more than enough tenderness for her children to balance the rage she feels when anyone threatens them."

—Claire's Reviews

"Matheson deftly illustrates the love of a mother for her children and the relationship between a mother and her stepchildren..."
　　—Karla "Bookish Life

"Matheson skillfully intertwines traditional Irish folklore with contemporary themes, creating a narrative that's both enchanting and relatable."
　　—Erik McManus, Breakeven Books

"Matheson did a wonderful job incorporating unique elements into this story while still staying true to the source material! ... You're going to find this story extremely riveting until the very last page!"
　　—Shawn, Mr Geek Book Reviews

CHRISTY MATHESON

the Horned Women

A Contemporary Retelling of an Irish Fairy Tale

THE CASTLE IN KILKENNY: FAIRY TALES BOOK 1

Also by Christy Matheson

The Castle in Kilkenny Fairy Tales

Book 1: *The Horned Women,*
A contemporary retelling of an Irish fairy tale

Book 2: *The White Deer of Kildare*

Book 3: *The Knight of the Terrible Valley and Aiden of Florida*

Book 4: *The Squire and His Magical Library*

Book 5: *The Knight and His Magical Armlet*

Book 6: *The Boat on the Lake of Regret*

Book 7: *Oona and the Swan*

Book 0.5: *The Leprechaun and the Castle* (only available through author's newsletter)

Magical Libraries (only available through author's newsletter)

In *Feisty Deeds: Historical Fictions of Daring Women,* "The Inner Good"

Contents

Dedication

To everyone who has ever been a thirteen-year-old girl or loved a thirteen-year-old girl, and most of all, to my own girls who are no longer thirteen.

I have full confidence in you.

The Dorned Women

I finish stoking the fire and push myself to my feet, slowly, as though I were already a crone. I haven't gotten nearly enough done for today, but that's the way it always is now. The workmen have gone home—leaving the back stairs half-finished and the plumbing main off—the little kids are blessedly asleep, the kitchen is tidy, and I can finally sit down. Maybe I can mend the kids' uniforms quickly and steal a few minutes to work on my beaded embroidery.

I let my gaze travel around the room, still not quite believing this is real, that I belong in a building so full of history and myth. Walls of local sandstone tower beyond the glow of the lamps, faded tapestries, coats of arms. This is the oldest part of the castle, and some nights I can almost hear the whisper of the generations that have come before me, all the way to when this was a wooden fort.

Despite my exhaustion, I can't help but smile. After all this—quitting grad school, Roy's "situations" leading to an entire year of divorce proceedings—and just look at me now. A little nobody from South Boston, and the sole proprietor of a castle. A castle! Dating from the medieval period, and still livable. Almost.

I reach for my mending—wait. I haven't locked the front door, and there's four children in the house. Pulling my sweater close, I hurry beyond the warm radius of the fire. The hallway angles slightly, and then I can see the entryway light and feel the draft whisking under my skirt. Is that noise nearby? Like laughter, or the trilling of a lark or a violin—I pause with my hand on the latch of the peep-out door. I'm already chilly, and that will just let in a blast of cold air and rain, when it's almost certainly just an owl or a truck driving past. I'll put the crossbar in its jambs, and then no matter what's out there, it can't come in. I pull my hand from where it is tucked in my sweater to reach for the heavy oak bar, and am startled by the clatter of tumbling glass.

"Hey Mum, are you down here?" Aidan calls.

Drat.

"Coming!" I hurry towards the kitchen before the teens break something else. The castle floor plan has kitchens and sculleries and still-rooms in the wing to my left, but I need a National Trust grant to restore them. Or something; yet another thing I haven't had time to research. Meanwhile, there's a useable kitchen shoehorned into one corner of the Great Hall.

I open the door. Aiden is picking up pieces of broken mason jars we use for drinking and dropping them in the bin, his younger sister Kaylee is standing in the middle of the floor glowering at her phone, and the kettle is whistling. I switch off the burner so the chaos dims a little. So much for my tidy kitchen! I've gotten my own kids to bed, but apparently I've got two more to deal with.

"Hey, Mum." Aiden stumbles over the word, his smile awkward. He pulls the cuffs of his Seattle Seahawks sweatshirt over his hands.

"Hi," I say, trying to sound cheerful. I appreciate the thought, but I am not his mum. When we lived in the US he called me Maura—if he had to call me anything—but I assume he wants to fit in with his Irish classmates. "Needed a midnight snack, I guess?"

"It isn't midnight," Kaylee argues.

"Okay." I take a breath. Here we go again. "You're right, it's not."

"Ugh, where did it go?" Kaylee is talking to her phone.

Her long blonde hair glimmers under the dull kitchen lighting, reminding me forcibly of Roy's first wife. Unlike her mother, Kaylee's roots are starting to show under her highlights. Since we've moved to Ireland, I've had no time to find a hair salon to maintain her look...although come to think of it, Kaylee hasn't asked me to go.

"It's 9:43," Aiden says, as though the precise time could avoid further conflict. He clunks the bin back in the corner and picks up his plate, containing ice cream and the last piece of apple cake.

That's fine. I made the cake for eating. I can always make another one.

I sweep up the last shards of glass from the floor. Don't want the little ones cutting their feet in the morning. Then I fetch the rag and wipe up the circles of ice cream that the carton left on the counter, then scrape the cake dish into the trash and stack it in the sink. Too bad the workmen turned off the downstairs water main so they can fix the bathroom, so I can't wash anything tonight. It makes me grumpy, watching tomorrow's chores add up, and I reach for Aiden's cup.

"Hey, Mum?" Aiden flushes with the too-easy blush that I know he abhors. "We can get that. You're not our servant."

That niggles, because in some ways, I do still feel like a servant around Roy's family—and even though they came with me, his older kids still feel part of his world. But I'm trying not to let my ex loom over me anymore, so I brush off the feeling and try to make a joke. "You'd think a place this big would come with staff, wouldn't you?" I laugh, but Aiden's smile barely twitches. "Maybe some magical ones, right?"

Aiden glances around the room. "Like...the teapots in *Beauty and the Beast?*"

There are serpentine gargoyles carved into the rafters, but the only teapots are the ones I bought from the homeware department at Dunnes.

"Something like that." I dump the last of his cocoa in the sink and stack the cup.

"I want a lamp to clean my room," Kaylee says, without looking at us.

I have a degree in comp lit and half a doctorate in folklore; I don't know how I ended up with children whose mythology comes from Disney.

I don't know how any of this happened. Me in Ireland with Roy's first four children, while he skips off to have his fifth. I wish his new wife the luck of him.

"Kaylee wants to make that." Aiden points his fork at his sister.

Still glowering, Kaylee holds her phone towards me, an Instagram video flickering. "It's pudding. See? In a mug."

Now they're both watching me, but I'm not sure what they're waiting for.

"Can she...make it?" Aiden's voice wavers.

"Of course." I've never given them any indication to think they can't use the kitchen, for Pete's sakes! "What do you need? Flour? Baking soda or powder?"

Kaylee reads the ingredients out loud, and I gather the dry ingredients and find a microwave-safe mug. I wait to see if she wants any other help, but she props up her phone and starts scooping and pouring. The tinny voice walks us all through the recipe over and over as Kaylee stops and starts the video.

"How is chemistry?" I ask Aiden. It seems like the sort of thing a good mother would ask.

"It's way harder than back in Florida," he answers, and stumbles through more details.

I nod and mm-hm. I don't know why they aren't both still in Florida. I can't help but glance at Kaylee, who hates the rain and has a constant sniffle and is embarrassed by wearing a school uniform. She hates the dark and all the corners around the castle are dark; we have dozens of lights on those chunky timers, and she also hates the cold so she keeps the space heater in her bedroom going full blast, and I don't complain even though electricity is wicked expensive here. By the end of a long day—and they're all long—I can barely remember why I wanted to move out here, and I have never had any idea why Aiden and Kaylee chose to come with me.

"Dammit!" Kaylee slams the microwave door.

Aiden and I both jump.

Kaylee bangs the mug on the counter, smoke pouring out.

She crosses her arms, glowering.

She sniffs.

It might be that her nose is running because of the cold, or because of the constant dust or the black sugary smoke. But that might be a wee quiver of her chin, and she might be feeling sad. Thirteen is still a child, I remind myself every day.

"You can try it again," I suggest, trying to sound positive.

"I can't. The cup's ruined."

"I'll wash it. Look, here's another mug."

Kaylee restarts the video. My mother would have said, 'if you keep looking like that your face will get stuck that way,' but it was never very helpful so I resist saying it to Kaylee.

As usual, I can't find anything to say to Kaylee. After all, she never says anything to me.

I start folding a basket of rags and towels, making stacks on the chrome-and-formica table. My knees hurt from standing all day, but I might as well do something useful while I'm waiting for the second round of pudding.

Aiden jostles the camping jug on the counter, making an echoing empty slosh. "Oh, sorry, I forgot to refill this. Do you want me to fetch water now?"

He opens the back door, the one that goes directly into the courtyard with the well, and a strange feeling slides down my spine. It is just an owl; no one is laughing out there.

"It's raining," Kaylee says.

"We can wait till morning," I answer.

Aiden nods and closes the door. I fold another towel, feeling silly for letting the night get to me.

"Thank you, though." It sounds like an afterthought, but I mean it. Not being able to use the kitchen sink is a huge frustration, but at least Aiden can carry in a bigger tub than I can manage, and he has been willing to help... if I remind him.

Aiden checks the kettle on the stove, and the soup pot next to it. "There's water in both? I think that's enough? Are you going to want tea?"

"It's fine." I laugh weakly. "I'm just one person; I don't need more tea than fits in the kettle." At this rate, I'm won't have time to stitch and sip anything, anyway.

"Oh, shi—oot!" Kaylee stabs her second pudding and stomps her foot. "It's all *globby!* And weird! And it smells bad!"

"You can make another one." Aiden sounds much more encouraging than I did.

Will I have to stand here through another whole pudding? For pity's sake, Oona is only six and she can microwave her own oatmeal, and Oliver often mixes up pancake batter while I cook. I don't know how Kaylee is managing to ruin five-ingredient pudding.

I touch my pocket, thinking I will find an easier recipe, but I left my phone upstairs, playing a sleepy-time meditation for Oliver. Never mind. I just get a new mug, and Kaylee turns her video back on. Aiden stands by the window, drumming his fingers.

"You don't have to get the water," I repeat. To be honest, I kind of don't want him out there at night. My grandmother always used to talk about the second sight, but Roy scoffed at such things; I'd almost forgotten the shivers I used to have—visceral reminders of a different world layered on top of our own, as soft as shadows.

But last week, Oliver wanted to fill his own water bottle directly from the well. He took his flashlight but came back saying that he couldn't find the spigot or any of the stainless steel pump housing that sits on top of the old stone circle. There was just a bucket, he told us, white with the rim painted black. Kaylee told him he was stupid and I said to watch her language, and soon Oona was wailing and Kaylee stomping, and that was before the workmen turned off the pipes so I just filled Oliver's water bottle from the sink and forgot about it.

But maybe we should fetch water in the daytime, just to be safe.

Out in the Great Hall, the grandfather clock strikes ten.

"Didn't I shut that thing down?" Aiden says. "It wakes up Oona." The deep chimes resonate up the grand staircase to the wing where the little children are sleeping.

"It rings every night at midnight," Kaylee answers. "Just midnight."

"How can a clock ring once a day?" Aiden asks. "I mean, just wondering."

I do not care about their squabbling. I'm folding a towel and watching the green numbers on the microwave, counting down as my pleasant solo sewing time disappears. Single parenting my own kids is hard enough, I didn't ask for two more. I put away the hand towels, unable to stop from slamming the cupboard door.

Kaylee snaps open the microwave.

"Did your pudding come out any better this time?" I manage to smile.

Kaylee shrugs. "Maybe. We're out of milk so I can't try again." She clatters through the drawer and pulls out a spoon. "That was fun."

She meanders out of the kitchen without meeting my eyes. I am not sure if that comment is mocking me or she means it. She didn't act like she was having fun.

Almost done. I wipe up the flour and sugar all over the counter. Not because I'm a servant, just because I want the kitchen done and the kids in bed.

"Are you fixing the kids' uniforms tonight?" Aidan asks.

"Yes." I shake the rag in the sink.

"Could you...could you fix something for me? It's just little. Nothing much."

I shouldn't take my mood out on Aiden. "Of course."

"Really? 'Cause, if you don't mind, you could do like you did on that gray skirt of yours. The kids all like it."

I'm surprised. "The one with all the colors? Visible mending?"

He nods, flustered but hopeful. He pulls his denim jacket from a chair under the table, where he clearly stashed it waiting for me.

"That's fine." I take the jacket and finger the rip, deciding what I can do. I put my hand on the light switch, waiting for Aiden to come towards the door. "Ready?"

"Um...yeah. But..." He pulls out another jacket, this one cream and soft gold. "Kaylee also wanted a bee? Like those ones you did on the pillowcases? She put a safety pin in the spot she wanted."

If Kaylee wanted a bee on her jacket, Kaylee could possibly manage to compile a complete sentence, look me in the eyes, and say it.

"Um...if it's okay? It would be really cool." He gives me that tentative smile. "Please?"

I take it and manage not to sigh. "Of course. I'm happy to do a bee." It means I won't get to my own project tonight, but maybe stitching will work its magic, filling me with positive thoughts while I work, binding her heart to mine.

We walk out of the kitchen together, saying goodnight, and Aiden heads towards the grand staircase while I turn towards the living room. I stoke the wood stove again, and settle in my comfortable, cozy, wonderful chair. Bliss!

I'll save the fun sewing for last. I pull out Oona's uniform and start pinning. My mind can wander as my fingers adjust the seams for her narrow torso, and I fall into daydreams. Oona adores being in Senior Infants, in the same school with her brother, and her anxious habits are fading. Oliver is anxious about fitting in, but Oona is making friends easily for the first time in her life. I worried that leaving her father would make her cling to me even more, but I think she has intuited that we are safe here. The waist and side seams close under my needle, and I have only the hem to finish.

"Open, open!" someone calls, and I am half out of my chair when I realize the sound is from the front hall, not bedroom wing. It must be—

My stomach plummets. I don't know who it could be. One of our neighbors, with some kind of country trouble? Footsteps clatter towards the living room, so I suppose I forgot to lock the door. What if—

A woman clumps into the shadows on the far side of the Great Hall and I am flooded with relief. She has a bag under one arm, a bulky sweater, and looks so normal and unthreatening compared to the visions that leapt into my mind. I'm not sure why she would just walk in, but I have to remember that this isn't an American city filled with high crime. Neighbors probably walk into each other's houses all the time here.

"Welcome," I say with a blank smile, falling back on habit since I'm discombobulated. Roy brought home a lot of odd friends. "Did you need help with something?"

The woman glances at me and flops into the chair by the fire. I think her name is Mrs Doherty, who lives down the road and we met at the church craft fair. She is tall and frowning, with scraggly gray hair and—

Is that a horn sticking out of her disheveled bangs? But of course it's October, so it might be a Halloween costume, although usually it's just the children who dress up here...

Whatever is happening here, no good comes from starting an argument, so I smile again. I've gotten good at acting nice while I was married to Roy, no matter how I felt inside.

The probably-Mrs. Doherty glowers at me as she snatches items from her bulky sack. Maybe it's a hat, like the visors with room for a ponytail, or a headband under her hair. She's got so much hair, it certainly could hide one. I catch myself staring and drop my eyes to the brushes in her hands.

This is familiar ground. I can talk about this, and maybe everything will make sense in a moment. "Oh, you've brought over some carding? It's always more pleasant to craft with company, isn't it?" I try to smile. If I act like everything is calm and normal, hopefully she will act calm and normal as well. If I stay calm, she won't bother the children. "I do love working with natural fibers." I hope she will respond, but she just pulls at her batt so I keep chattering. "I tried carding, too, a few years ago. I found local wool, and learned all the steps to card and spin it. I didn't have enough for weaving, but I knitted a baby sweater. Have you watched the Sheep to Shawl competition? Amazing, isn't it..."

Okay. I don't actually think this is my new neighbor Mrs. Doherty. And I'm really not sure about that horn. All the more reason to stay composed.

"Where are the women?" not-Mrs.-Doherty snaps, staring towards my front door. "They delay too long!"

What women? Oh—I suppose it might be a craft circle. That would explain why she didn't greet me, because I'm sewing and she thought I was part of the circle too. It's the second Wednesday in October, and it's perfectly possible that some local women have used this castle for their crafting club on the second Wednesday of every month for years. Why not? I've already noticed that the whole neighborhood has a proprietary feeling about the castle, which I understand completely. Roy's money bought the property, but it's their history. Hosting a craft circle is a great way to give back to the community, really; I just wish I had known about it ahead of time. And maybe had some input about the meeting time.

Or maybe I'm dreaming it all? Maybe my imagination finally did run away with me. Or I fell asleep mending.

Before I can introduce myself, there is more clattering, heavy shoes on flagstones, something dragging. I really thought I had locked the door, but that must have been last night. Or wait, I remember reaching out, but then the mason jars fell.

"Welcome," I say as the second woman enters. My voice comes out tentative.

They must be meeting in costume. That's a perfectly rational explanation for... more horns? Maybe it's a theme?

The second woman ignores my greeting and snaps, "Give me place!"

Did I lock the door or did I not? Did I go to the kitchen before or after the bar fell into place? My armpits prickle and I can smell my own sour, anxious sweat. Why didn't I lock the door?

I gesture towards the sofa, but the second woman thumps her spinning wheel down next to the first. I drop my eyes to Oona's uniform, trying not to stare. This woman is short and neatly dressed, her hair pulled into a smooth bun, so there is nothing hiding her forehead.

Nothing to hold those two horns in place.

Two!

This is more than Halloween or a strange call in the dark or a whispery feeling on my spine. Although come to think of it, if I stop filling my head with justifications, I have a lot of whispery feelings on my spine, and everywhere else. I try to use that way of relaxing my vision that used to work as a child, but I come up with nothing. I've been in Roy's world for too long...

Cringing under the memory of his chuckles, once again feeling helpless and useless, I say nothing as the third woman enters. Three horns and a lap loom, and she draws up a stool next to the spinning woman, even though I don't keep stools in the living room. Roy would come up with a logical explanation, and he would laugh at me for being afraid of old women.

"Open, open!" calls a new voice, thin and reedy. I recognize the sound of the wooden bar lifting, although it's on the inside of the house and none of us are near the door.

I must be dreaming. Making up problems that don't exist, like Roy often accused me.

But the draft when the door opens is real. The swoosh of a car on the highway is like every other night. This is definitely Oona's uniform, with the same chalk marks I used this afternoon. And if everything else is real, maybe these are not ordinary women, maybe—

A low voice calls to my door as the fourth woman takes out wooden knitting needles.

Maybe these women have been having their craft circle here for a very long time. Centuries.

If they are real, what do I do next? My heart is pounding with fear, but they haven't actually done anything bad. They haven't attempted to pass beyond the Great Hall and do anything to the children. If my instincts are right and Roy's mocking is wrong, then these are fae—and the Irish fae are often demanding but not always evil.

The fifth woman comes in. She has five horns and a drop spindle.

And if Roy were right and the fae are only in my imagination, there are still more of them than me. I couldn't physically force them to leave my house, and I'm told if we call 999 to expect it to take an hour or more out here. Besides, I left my phone next to Oliver. I'm not going to go fetch it; it's definitely a better idea to keep an eye on these women.

Not daring to make a fuss, I return to Oona's hem. The door thumps and clatters, and seven more women file into my living room, one—by—one. Each has a tool for working wool, and each has one more horn than the last. Pretending to keep my eyes on my thread as I knot it off, I count twelve horns bristling from the forehead of the woman nearest me.

I don't know what to do, so I rethread my needle and mend Oliver's school pants. My son snagged it while sliding down the hill getting covered in dirt. Like children do. Normal second graders, in normal schools. I stitch and listen, listen and stitch.

I have to decide what to do next.

The women mumble short comments to each other, perhaps in Irish or perhaps I am just too unsettled to decipher their accents. I don't understand, but this is definitely real. The women make the room smell of wool and fennel, bump into a picture frame and send it clattering to the floor, make a breeze when they flap out their skirts to sit. Speaking of sitting, I arranged this big drafty room with only two recliners, a little rocker for Oona, and one couch, which is enough seating for one woman and four children. Now there are twelve people—plus me—seated in a circle, and all of them have chairs and stools.

The clock whirrs and the chimes strike eleven. Startled, I stare at Oliver's pants, which are somehow already finished, my familiar stitches making neat rows up and down them. I know sewing is meditative, but the last hour seemed to just vanish.

Since there is nothing else to sew, I knot the final stitch and snip my thread. I am tempted to sit and stitch all night, staring into the fire and waiting for someone to tell me what to do. I need to take some sort of action and wake myself up from this odd daze.

"Would you care for some tea, perhaps?" I speak over-loudly, since none of my guests have acknowledged me yet.

Twelve heads turn and twelve pairs of eyes stab into me.

"Yes, mistress," says the first woman. "Go fetch it."

"Gladly." I smile as I rise. If tea will keep them content, I will make as much tea as they can drink. Fortunately my chair is closest to the kitchen, so I do not have to move any closer to them.

I flick the kitchen switch, relieved when the lightbulbs turn on in the usual way, even though one is bright white and one is more yellow and ordinarily that irritates me. I take a slow breath, annoyed that it trembles as I exhale. I yearned to move to Ireland because I loved the folklore so much: another layer of truth exists next to our world, sometimes separate and sometimes touching. There's no reason to be upset just because what I have always believed has turned out to be true.

I have always imagined that the stories were real, so it isn't the fae themselves that worry me. It's having them in the house with my children.

I turn on the gas under the kettle and the pot, blowing on the burner that's always stubborn to light. As I fetch trays and mugs and teapots, my mind seems to clear. The Irish canon rewards bravery, cleverness, and obedience to the elder's wisdom. There are twelve horned women in my living room, and I just need to keep them away from my children. That's all. So I'll ply them with tea, keep the fire warm–and keep my eye on them.

I put sugar bowls on the trays, but we're out of cream. Maybe they won't notice. The kettle whistles, and I turn off the burner, but the pot isn't boiling yet.

The Irish canon also rewards a mother's love and loyalty, and that much I can do. In this dragged-out divorce, I have been through every shame and accusation, and weathered them for the sake of my children. I have been through fire for Oona and Oliver, and I am hot with certainty that we will get through this night safely, too.

Think, Maura. I have a dozen horned women in my living room. There are two possibilities here: one, these are wise crones, and showing them gratitude and hospitality will pave the way for their wise advice. Or two—

In the living room, the women start singing, their voices darting under and over, shrill and canting. I find myself scooping herbs from a ceramic pot with no recollection of the last few minutes or where this pot came from. I shake my head, hard, and start singing "Hallelujah" by Leonard Cohen. Oona has been obsessed with it lately, although Kaylee rolls her eyes and makes fun of her, and I let her alternate the playlist with Taylor Swift. I sing some of that, too, with a little shimmy. Nice and twenty-first century.

I tip the kettle over the herbs, and they bloom into a bright red color. I stare, and stare...

I shake my head hard, turning away from the acrid smell and forcing myself to start singing again. My thoughts move more freely again.

Option two is looking more and more likely. These are evil fae. The crones, the mother, and the innocent—my job in this story is to keep these horned women away from my children.

The children, the children, the children.

As I carry the trays back to the Great Hall, I barricade my mind with memories of my children.

The night when Oliver was born and my whole world was filled with color that I had never known. And Oona's birth; the pain, the ecstasy, Roy holding us both.

I remember us kicking leaves as we walked through the park, one sticky little hand in each of mine. Oona's laugh as I pushed her on the swing, up to the moon, visit the stars. Oliver's face when he brought me home a holiday-themed glob of construction paper and popsicle sticks, and then later with spelling tests and double-digit addition.

My memories fortify me all the way around the circle of horned women, pouring tea and passing mugs.

Twelve, sitting in order from one horn to twelve. I must keep them here, far from Oona and Oliver. I let my love throb, and I feel so strong and clear-headed that I have faith I will be able to protect them.

They do not speak to me, so I settle back in my chair to keep an eye on them. I pick up my mending, and the fuzzy texture surprises me. I blink, startled. This isn't a primary school uniform.

It's Burberry wool, one denim sleeve flopping out from underneath. Kaylee and Aiden! I forgot them entirely!

My heart sinks. Four children to care for, and I don't have years of love for my stepchildren, who aren't even really my official stepchildren. Resentment boils through the thoughts tumbling into my mind.

They are old enough to take care of themselves. I should focus on the little ones.

We all know what stepmothers are like. If I'm stuck in a folk tale, there's no point in me trying to be good.

If I forgot them already, then it must mean my love—tepid and hesitant at best—isn't going to be enough to protect them anyways.

Suddenly, I'm hot and angry with guilt. How could I forget them, even momentarily? I didn't ask for Aidan and Kaylee to live with us, but I thought I was trying my best. Apparently my best isn't much good.

Worst of all, I can't help thinking that if things get worse, maybe I could give Kaylee to the witches. Maybe that sacrifice would be enough to save the other children. And even more worst of all, the idea of that gives me a rush of pleasure, as though any part of this is a competition and any part of me would relish victory over a thirteen-year-old.

This is awful! I don't have to give in to thoughts like these.

I flatten one hand across the cream-and-gold wool and pick through my embroidery threads. I did a whole set of bees for the pillowcases last year and my fingers know how to do this practically without thought, which is just as well. I need my wits if we're all to survive this night.

I am determined that we all survive this night, including Kaylee. If a stepmother must betray her children, then I must rewrite that story.

I thread my needle and backstitch an oval for the bee's body. Some of the women are humming now, someone laughs, the spinning wheels whirr, and my mind is blurry.

It helped to hold onto memories of the little ones, so I need happy memories of Kaylee now. It isn't easy to keep her close to my heart, but I'm an intelligent woman. More to the point, Roy has spent years teaching me how to keep myself guarded. If I know that, I can also choose to open the gates to my heart. It might not be easy to love Kaylee, but I can make the choice to do it.

Until this month, I've mostly only seen the older kids at Thanksgiving, one week in the Bahamas every February and two weeks at the lake house every July. My mind flickers through Kaylee picking a fight with toddler Oliver, Kaylee scrolling her phone during a dinner I spent hours making, Kaylee demanding that her dad buy her some expensive gadget.

No. Is it the witches making me think like this? Surely I can do better. My fingers fly back and forth, filling the bee with bright golden satin stitch. That's when I notice that there are no piles of batts next to the carders; the spools on the spinning wheels are not growing fat; the traditional crios belts are not extending from the loom and snaking towards the floor.

I wrap the thread on my needle and plunge it above for a pistil stitch, then a second, and raise it to my eyes. I rub it. Yes, there are two cute little antennae. Yes, the whole bee is now yellow.

We are all crafting, but I am the only one in this room who is creating something.

I have a whole repertoire of fancy stitches for my bees, but right now I just choose simple and quick. The horned women can influence my thoughts, but they can't change the fabric so I must sew my love for Kaylee into her jacket. Do I love Kaylee? No time to think of that now. I load two needles with black thread and work quickly, filling in stripes and outlining wings. The witches are murmuring among each other, and I can feel resentment pummeling me. Kaylee told her mother about all my working-class gaffes. Roy only took a few days of vacation a year, but Kaylee demanding all his attention. Kaylee sniggering about how much weight I gained after Oona was born, and Roy giving her all my designer dresses, which were one thing he bought for me, one thing he liked about me, and then Kaylee spilled sauce poivrade all over the yellow one.

I stitch faster and let the thoughts fly past like gnats, annoying but insignificant. They do not define Kaylee, and I will not let them define me.

I take a few careful stitches in silver-white, suggesting the wings and defining the rump. One last tiny stay stitch.

Simultaneously, I snip my thread—

"Mistress," says the Woman of One Horn—

And I realize that although I have never witnessed Kaylee being kind, neither have I witnessed an adult being kind to her. There's something—

"Make us a cake," orders One-Horn, and I find myself rising to my feet. I cannot stop from walking into the kitchen and reaching for my biggest bowl. I resent the horned women's interference, for I wouldn't be foolish enough to disobey twelve witches. Those fairy tales never end well.

Which story are we in? Perhaps if I keep them busy until dawn, they must leave and my children will be safe.

Or perhaps I must sanctify. I stack the cake pans and bless them in the name of the Father and the Son and the Holy Ghost. The Christian gods have been in Ireland for a long time, but it doesn't feel quite right. I scoop flour and think of Demeter, the harvest. Yes; this is a women's story. The mother and the crone. Isis, be with us, I whisper to the eggs. Izanami, raise my family with this baking soda. Freyja, love as sweet as this sugar and my husband's tongue on the night we conceived. My spoon circles: Asase Yaa, Umay, Frigg; protect my children. Mór Muman, this is your butter, your land, and I am a mother as you are a mother. I turn on the oven; Pelehonuamea, burn the evil from my hearth.

I stare at the batter, gloopy and dense, and cannot think of any more names. I suppose I was making a simple cottage pudding, something I have often thrown together during one episode of Octonauts. But it needs liquid.

I open the avocado-colored fridge, but the milk jug is empty. Oh yes; Kaylee and her microwave puddings. Just water will do.

I hold the measuring cup under the tap and spin the handle for a whole minute before I remember the main is turned off.

The kettle—is empty. The pot. I jiggle the camping jug. I have forgotten something. The jug, what about the jug?

Aiden! Aiden is the one who fills the jug. And I had forgotten about him entirely. Entirely!

I am filled with a sick sense of foreboding. My throat is parched, and I tip the jug forward so the last bit pours into my glass. I drink it down, this water that Aiden has fetched for me, and try to make some sense out of this jumble.

The horned women are busy but make nothing. The opposite of their bitterness is acceptance; the opposite of their barrenness is creation.

There it is—I have mended the clothing for three of my children. I have stitched down my feelings for them, and even Kaylee is perfectly clear to me now. I see the little tremble of her chin when her pudding came out wrong, and I see now that she didn't dare ask me for help because her own mother never even let her try.

The witches compelled me into the kitchen this time. Their hold on me is growing, and I am flushed and shaking with the knowledge that I must complete Aiden's mending before they make their next move. Eating is a spell of its own; I have a bad feeling about this cake.

Hands stumbling, I bang the pans and scrape the top of the bowl, leaving the floury blob. I open the oven door (it creaks) and slam it closed.

Head down, I shuffle back to the living room. "Mothers, your cake is baking," I tell them.

They squeal and chitter with anticipation, and I slink back into my chair. Aidan's coat. I must finish his repair before they notice my deception.

I do not look up while I sew this time. I choose my threads quickly: pale blue like Aiden's eyes, turquoise like the sea outside the Florida mansion where he grew up, deep blue for the pure water he fetches for me. My heart is pounding, but my hands know this work and do not tremble or dawdle. When I finish a running stitch around the tear, I bring the denim to my face to check the sewing. I breathe in the smell of Aiden: fresh air, Sublime Gold shampoo, his own musky sweat. I am ashamed that he has been calling me 'Mum' for almost a month and I have never held him close enough to know his smell.

I feel the witches' influence tug at my mind as I slide the patch and darning egg under the denim. Aiden ruined sneakers on the second time out, sneakers so expensive they could have paid for my college wardrobe.

Aiden warning Oliver about all the ways he wouldn't be popular in kindergarten and making him cry. Aiden throwing up for one entire trip to Hawaii, until I couldn't wash the smell off my hands and—

Hey. This is ridiculous. Who could resent a child for vomiting?

With my ground stitches in place, it's time to add running stitches over the top in all the different blues I have chosen. Blend it together. Repair the damage. Mend what you can, Maura.

My brain is bleary with magic and stress and also plain exhaustion. Has the clock struck midnight yet? Oona always wakes me by six.

I don't have enough memories of Aiden to weave into his coat. He's always been quiet, gone into his room or played on his Switch when Roy started raising his voice. I know I must weave in my memories to hold tight to my love, so I pull out the heavy artillery, the memory that always makes my heart pound and my throat tight, even when there are not twelve horned women in my living room:

My divorce from Roy took an entire year, and we had to appear in court again and again. It is not that I am litigious. It was because Roy had not properly finalized his first divorce, and she was claiming his assets and Roy had a new pregnant girlfriend to care for as well. And his money is all family wealth so his brother was involved as well. The way I was raised, the whole thing was shameful, so I retreated into myself and held onto two requests only: I wanted full custody of Oliver and Oona, and I wanted a castle in Ireland.

That last demand sounded foolish, even to me who had dreamed of it all my life. But Roy really owns a great deal of property, and I was entitled to a great many parts of it. Since no one could decide who owned how much of all these houses and companies, they were delighted that I would cede my share in exchange for a single solitary property. My lawyer insisted that Roy throw in necessary furniture and upkeep for thirty-five years. But even once that was sorted, I still had to sit there while Roy argued with his first wife and his brother, and his girlfriend cried dramatically and the judge rubbed his temples. And then on what we all hoped would be the final day, the judge went down all the custody agreements one last time.

Roy's lawyer and my lawyer had worked them out amicably in mediation. I thought there were no surprises.

I was knitting on a side bench, my braid frazzled and my jacket creased from Oona's clinging tantrum when I left her at kindergarten, trying to appear politely uninterested in the endless bickering. Roy's older kids entered the court room, accompanied by no fewer than four women in designer suits and perfect hair.

"So, um, yeah," Aiden addressed the judge. "You said we were old enough to make our own choice. This time. Um, your Honor."

Kaylee trailed behind, examining the sparkles on her nails. I never know what she is thinking.

"That's right, young man," the judge answered, his pen ready. "Do you want to maintain the current arrangement?"

Aiden scratched his ear. "We'll both go with Maura," he said. "Full time. Um, yeah."

The entire courtroom went so silent that you could have heard a butterfly's wings unfurl.

One of the women with them clicked forward, perfectly poised in wholly impractical four-inch heels. "I'm their psychiatrist. I have discussed this at length with both siblings. Here is my report supporting the decision that Aiden just announced to Your Honor."

And then everything erupted. Back then, I was too numb to feel anything at all. Now, I go over the memory every night before I fall asleep, and the part I hold close is when Aiden glanced around the courtroom, panic growing in his too-young face, until his eyes met mine.

I kept my expressions shuttered back then. But Aiden had seen something, and he smiled, just a little, and he hugged his arms close to himself, just a smidge. And he made it through that awful afternoon, repeating his words every time he was asked.

I'm going with Maura. I'm going with Maura. I'm going with Maura.

"Where's our cake?" screeches One-Horn.

"I don't smell a thing," complains Two-Horn.

"Is the mistress lazy?" demands Three-Horn.

I stab my stay-stitch, slide the needle under, and snip my thread before I speak. It isn't my best work, but Aiden's jacket is mended. I can feel him now, his tentative smile, the way we are finding things to laugh about together, the way he brings me his literature homework and asks me questions with trust in his eyes.

It is not just Aiden I am feeling, it is us. A relationship that I didn't even realize belonged to me.

"Good mothers, let me fetch it," I answer, rising to my feet, eyes cast downwards. I rush to the kitchen, their hackling chasing me down the passage. I have a scant few seconds to come up with an excuse or a lie.

I slam the door behind me, my eyes scanning the kitchen desperately. Every mythology has its own central themes, its own types of warnings and its own particular unhappy endings. The thing is, the Irish canon is particularly bad about children.

It is bad about the fae stealing children, and there are twelve fae in my living room while my four children sleep upstairs. I must make the right choices, but there are as many stories as there are story-tellers, and there is no way to know which one I am in.

Kaylee's pudding. The microwave. Maybe I can cook up the cake really fast.

I dart across the kitchen, but as my hand tugs the microwave's handle, sparks begin to fly. Its lights all flash, randomly, frenetically. I slam the door and back away. It isn't unexpected that electricity doesn't work right—

Then the entire microwave starts blinking and flickering. First with green light, then the whole thing disappears for a second, is back, gone and back and...gone. All that's left is a little puddle of grease on the counter.

"Dammit!" I swing my fist and thump the counter. Now I'm mad. This isn't abstract any more.

It's one thing to try and raise four children—all wealthy and American—in a drafty, half-ruined castle in Kilkenny. It's another to try to do it without a damn microwave! I'm going to be drinking lukewarm tea and eating lukewarm food for the rest of my life! How will Oona make her oatmeal packets for breakfast—

Never mind. We need to survive till breakfast time, which is looking uncertain. Enough with the microwave. Maybe I can just throw the batter in the oven, maybe in little pieces like cookies and it will cook faster.

But it's so cold in the kitchen that the butter didn't mix in properly, so the batter is mostly flour with globs where it's stuck to the egg. I set the whole bowl on the warm stove and beat that spoon as hard as I can.

The clock in the hallway whirrs, plays its song on out-of-tune chimes, and strikes the hour. Midnight. It is their time now.

"Mistress, is there a problem?"

The voice comes to me as clear as day, and when I look up I can see straight to the horned women. It is as though the wall between us is nothing but mist, or ice, or old-fashioned glass with its bubbles and waves.

"Where is our cake?" screeches Five-Horn, and my feet carry me back towards them as though I am a yo-yo, the bowl cradled in my arms.

Their magic does not compel my words, and I have an idea. "We are out of milk, and I have used the water for your tea. Is there any left? I can mix the batter with your tea."

Their eyes fixed on me, the three closest to the teapots each reach out an arm, lift the pot, and tip it over a cup. The pots are all empty, and the gestures all are in eerie synchronicity.

"Go fetch some water from the well," Six-Horn orders.

"Yes, mothers." I drop a fumbling curtsey, and am allowed to return to the kitchen. Okay, the well. I didn't want to leave the house with the witches and children inside, but the well is only a dozen steps from the kitchen doorway. The courtyard has castle walls on all four sides, built up over the centuries. This well has been here since before the time of Christ, and I have always liked it.

Okay. I can do this. I don't need to fill the whole heavy jug, I just need a couple of cups. Some for the cake, and some for my parched throat. I plonk the mixing bowl back on top of the stove and grab the teakettle.

The handle comes off in my hand and the kettle falls back onto the stove, breaking in half.

It's a metal kettle. This is not normal.

I use both hands to lift the pot, cautiously, but it shatters into a dozen pieces. Usually, my cheap clearance pots hang from wrought-iron hooks, but the hooks are empty. I open the cabinet with our dishes, only to find a heap of broken crockery. Same with my baking drawer. How about the low cupboard, with Oona's plastic cups—they're…gone.

Horned Women, with every passing minute I am liking you less and less.

We've barely moved in, so there's not much more to look for. I glance at the mixing bowl with the gloppy batter; I could take it outside and put it under the tap…

That gives me a bad feeling. A very bad feeling. I don't take the time to analyze it; I assume there is some folktale that my subconscious remembers. But it would be quick, I could run, I could make the cake. I must finish the cake!

I am holding the bowl and halfway to the door by the time I realize I am doing exactly what I decided against.

"No! Stop." I pause, twitching towards the door. Song works better; I figure out lyrics with the word "stop" and when I sing a couplet I am able to obey myself and set the bowl back down. I must trust myself.

Roy would laugh at me, but I am making the choices here. Not him. Not the witches.

That invisible string draws me back to the living room. Fine. They have some power. But I will hold onto my own.

"I have no vessel to fetch the water," I tell them.

"Take a sieve, and bring water in it," orders Seven-Horn.

I curtsey again, with a bubble of hope. There are dozens of stories about a sieve becoming solid once a supernatural creature tells a human to fetch water with it.

"And don't come back until you do!" she cries to my receding back, and the others all cackle and chortle.

The sieves in the stories were probably not like mine, faded green plastic with a too-long handle so the basket wobbles and sags when it is full. I slip on my fleece and shoes and carry my sieve to the well. Please, my children be safe. I'll be quick.

I find the flashlight in my fleece pocket and shine it up into the well, and find the bar and the crank and even the bucket with a painted rim just like Oliver described. But when I shine my light down, the water is sparkling only a little way below the top of the well. I don't need to figure out the pulleys and bucket, I can reach down and touch it.

As I draw in slow breaths, I realize how much the witches have clouded my mind. The air smells of wood smoke and elderberries, rotting leaves and wet stones. I close my eyes and look back to girlhood-Maura, the joyful confident Maura at Indiana University, the Maura who knew she could feel the shivers of the world that barely touches our own. I let my fingertips of my left hand trail in the water, and lift the other towards my children's bedrooms. Their lights are out, but I know they are there. Sleep little ones. Do not come downstairs tonight.

If I trust myself, I know that I love them. All four of them. I draw that love around me like a cloak, like the wisp of smoke when I blow out Kaylee's Lilly Pilly candle, fastened closed with one of Oona's sticky kisses.

I can feel that love, a spider-light thread from my fingertips to their hearts. The gray sandstone wavers, just a moment, and I recognize this shiver. I can feel their heartbeats.

Two heartbeats. I close my eyes and reach deeper, searching for Kaylee and Aiden.

I can still hear the witches in the Great Hall, which is the front side of this courtyard. Our bedrooms are upstairs in the second wing. The third side is falling apart; I asked the workers to nail boards across the entrance to our tower, because all four children want so badly to explore it. Behind me, the fourth wing is storerooms and garages.

I cup both hands in the water and drink. It is clean and sharp, like fine wine with the memories of herbs and minerals in the edges of the mouth. I drink again and again, four handfuls.

Come on, Maura! Four heartbeats! Find them all! Try harder!

I glance back towards the lighted living room. Although the sitting area is past the kitchen, I can almost see them, the silhouettes of women in dark gowns, their hands carding and spinning, the shadows of their horns dancing in the firelight. I need to act before they come outside and start making choices for me.

I dip the sieve in the well. All the water pours out, just like you would expect.

I dip it again and again. Try putting my hands over the bottom. Try wrapping my skirt underneath and running towards the kitchen door, but it only soaks my skirt and leaves the sieve empty. I try carrying water in my hands, which become frigid and stiff. I dig through my fleece pockets; maybe there's a plastic bag, a candy wrapper, something to block the holes, anything anything anything. I must be more clever than this trap they have set for me.

If I can dip water into the broken shards of a pot, I could fill the mixing bowl tablespoon by tablespoon. I turn back toward the kitchen, but my feet stick. I yank myself, but the momentum only knocks me to my knees, my palms hitting the flagstones and I cry out in pain, or maybe fear and despair and self-loathing. I cannot solve their puzzle, I cannot escape their trap.

The clock strikes one.

This is the deepest depth of the night; I have hours to keep them busy until dawn closes the gates between our worlds.

"It seems the mistress has forgotten us," says One-Horn.

When I raise my head, once again, it is as though I am looking through medieval glass, slightly distorted, but the light shines clearly. Except this time, I am also looking through my own tears.

"We must make the cake ourselves," says Two-Horn.

"If the mistress has no milk, then we will mix the cake with blood," says Three-Horn.

Damn Kaylee, damn her three stupid puddings and burning the edges and she didn't even share and now we are out of milk!

"I know where the children are," says Four-Horn.

"Maura, you're being foolish," I say aloud, pushing myself onto my knees. It's 2024; no one would ever think of saving enough milk to make a cake for witches in the middle of the night! And if anyone could think such a thing, it would be me, the folklorist, who knows something about saving milk. The teens only know Disney.

Besides, I'm the adult. I'm responsible.

"Let us go find them," says Five-Horn.

"They will be delicious," says Six-Horn, and they all rise.

"Stop!" I scream. I stagger onto my feet, but the only direction I can move is back to the well. "Stop! You may not pass! Stop!"

Unperturbed, they all file out of the Great Hall, into the corridor to the grand staircase that curves around both sides of the Elizabethan hall. Up the first seven steps. Like a ballet dance, they part, one taking the right and the next the left, in perfect unison.

"Stop!" I cry again, but my voice is weak and trembling. It is obvious that they do not hear or perhaps they just do not care.

The first witch draws a silver blade, the second a lamp, and the two lines reunite as one. This is the hallway that leads to the bedrooms. To my children.

I am responsible. Responsible for their lives, their innocence.

Roy's mother told me I couldn't do it, four children and a foreign country and me full of these useless ideas. My own mother said I would have another think coming, trying to parent without Roy's money solving all my problems. Aiden and Kaylee's mother said a dozen things, each worse than the last. No one wanted me here. No one trusted me.

I sag down on top of the stone wall. My hair is falling out of its braid, my legs shaking under my wet clothes, my numb fingertips trail in the water. The plastic sieve tumbles at my feet, as useless as I am.

Two-Horn opens the door to the big bedroom and One-Horn glides in, holding the blade above her head. I can see Oona now, sleeping on the right, and Oliver tucked into his bed on the left.

Wait. I can see. Through the walls.

This is some kind of magic. The Horned Women are not listening to me, but the house itself is. And that thread—that thread that I stitched between my children and myself—

I lift my hand, and I feel it. I breathe the air, I touch the stones and the water, and I can find my baby. There is Oona, not through a glass darkly, but her heartbeat as close as when she used to nurse at my breast.

Seven-Horn holds up a lantern, Eight-Horn pulls Oona's arm from beneath the blankets, and Nine-Horn kneels beside Oona's bed with a crystal bowl in her hands.

I have nothing to sew, but I must find my own strength. A song has power, a verse, a rhyme, but what can I say? I cannot command the witches. The house is too large, too old, for me to change. But perhaps I can command my children. Fly away? Fight? Those seem foolish.

One-Horn slashes her knife through the air, glinting in the lantern-light. The silver tip dives into my baby's wrist and red spurts onto One-Horn's white hand and drips into the bowl.

My baby, her blood—

"Child who was born to me, Do not let your blood run free..."

My words are tumbling and fumbling, a half-question at the end of the sentence. It's the way I have been talking to Roy for years now, trying to be kind, hoping to influence him. It's the way I talk to Aiden and Kaylee and the handyman. I hate it, I hate who I have become.

The Horned Women look up, as though they have noticed some presence besides themselves.

Oona's blood is still dripping, but it is no longer gushing.

I try again, stirring the well-water, gripping the stones, pulling anger and love into my lungs and transforming them into a clarion call.

"Child who was born to me,
Do not let your blood run free!"

Oona does not stir, but the drips slow, then stop. She lays as though a marble statue, but I can feel the torpid beat of her heart.

Nine-Horn holds up the bowl and the others inspect it.

"That is not enough for our cake," says Ten-Horn.

"We must collect more," says Eleven-Horn.

"Our cake must be a delicious feast," says Twelve-Horn.

"And we must have enough to share," says One-Horn, and she turns to Oliver's bed.

They move quickly, but this time I am prepared. It is terrible to watch one's child in pain, and I wince away as the blade pierces my sweet boy's tender skin. But I keep my gaze steady and I make my voice strong:

> *"Child who is born to me,*
> *Do not let your blood run free!"*

The dripping stops quickly, and they collect less blood than they got from Oona. Visibly irritated, they repeat their statements and head down the hallway.

I am too busy thinking to pay them much attention. I can say my rhyme before they get to Aiden, but obviously I cannot say the same thing. What power I have is rooted in love and in truth.

"Child who has chosen me, do not let your blood run free," I try, but I can feel that they are just words. My rhyme for Oona was yanked from my heart, from my womb.

"Child of my heart..." But he's not, we don't love each other yet. *"Child who I honor and respect..."* I'm never going to rhyme that. *"Child I swear to protect and defend..."* That has no meaning because I have given him nothing; nothing of my true self. I have dealt with school paperwork and folded his laundry, but I have guarded my heart. I have not even asked Aiden what he likes to have best for dinner.

Two-Horns opens Aiden's door. She does not know the way it always sticks and drags, and it takes her three tries to get inside.

One-Horn raises the knife above her head, but the blade is no longer shiny. It is dark with the blood of my children, and I am burning with anger. Aiden's face is sweet and young on the pillows, and he is such a good kid, and he chose to be here. No one else thought I was anything, but Aiden trusted me and this heat, this rage, this power emanates from the magma of the earth and radiates through my entire body—and this is love.

> *"Child who chose me, all above,*
> *Let me enwrap you in motherly love..."*

That is all true, it is all Aiden. My thread spools out and catches him, but now I need to say my truth for him. Except I do not know my own truth, not for these two children.

One-Horn plunges her knife into his arm, and Nine-Horn pushes her bowl closer. His blood splashes down. No no no, it is too fast, and I want—

> *"I want you beside me for days and for years,*
> *Do not shed blood and"*

—rhyme with years, rhyme with years—

> *"do not cry tears!"*

I'm not getting nominated for the next poet laureate, but the house or the air or their souls hear my passion, and his bleeding ceases.

"Is that enough?" asks Twelve-Horn.

"I want a good cake," says Eleven-Horn.

"There is one more child," says Ten-Horn, and they turn to file out of the room.

But my mind is racing faster than their dance-like pace, and Kaylee's room is down and around the corner. I'm getting the hang of this, but what is the truth for Kaylee? She did not choose me, I did not work for her. She is just—aha!

> *"Dear child who is broken,*
> *I am thankful you stayed,*
> *Each day I am grateful for the choice you have made."*

It catches her, like a bee flying from my fingertips and spooling the thread of my love around her. Poor Kaylee, who didn't want to leave her school and is chronically cold and scared of the dark, but every single adult in her life is even worse than this, and she just wants to make her pudding and I am enraged, irate, incensed that yet another person is trying to hurt her.

The Horned Women turn into her corridor, and Seven-Horn holds the lantern while Two-Horn reaches towards the door.

"Door!" I scream. *"Please hold fast!*

Lock! Fall in place!"

There is a thump and a clatter as Two-Horn shoves.

"Protect my sweet child from pain and disgrace!" I yell.

Two-Horn pulls and yanks, but the door does not budge. Nine-Horn blows on the lock. Eight-Horn kicks it. Seven-Horn searches up and down the hallways for a different entrance.

I am exultant, my heart pounding so hard I can hear the rush in my ears. I say the whole rhyme again, my voice quiet and steely, like the way I wish I presented myself to the world.

> *"Dear child who is broken,*
> *I'm thankful you stayed,*
> *Each day I am grateful for the choice you have made.*
> *Door! Please hold fast!*
> *Lock! Fall in place!*
> *Protect my sweet child from pain and disgrace."*

"We cannot get through," says Six-Horn.

"We have enough, though barely," says Five-Horn, examining the bowl.

"Let us go and bake our cake, our cake!" shrieks Four-Horn. They file away, and the walls grow dim then solid.

My children are safe, for now. But what happens once that cake is cooked?

I stand and test my feet. I can walk around the well, but I cannot leave it. I fill my hands and take a step away, but as soon as the water drains I am pulled back. Now I can see the Horned Women in the kitchen, but the normal way—through the window. I think they have forgotten me, but the compulsion she spoke earlier remains in place. Don't come back until you fetch the water. I am still trapped, but everything has changed. I have changed.

I am connected to something, and I speak to it. "How can I fetch this water?"

A woman's voice answers me, low and resonant. "Take my yellow clay and moss and bind them together, and plaster the sieve so it will hold."

This would seem like it is obvious, but I have only ever seen this courtyard with paving stones and pebbles and shiny steel. Hm, perhaps the moss was cleaned when they installed the pump? I walk around the well, shining my flashlight, dragging my fingertips into the corners and between the stones. It is well-worn stone, but I find bits of clay here and bits of moss there. Just enough to plaster the sieve. Slowly, but hopefully fast enough.

I dip the sieve in the well. Water drips but holds. I walk towards the house, one step, two, three, four. Twelve steps and I am at the door. The cake is baking and I pass through the empty kitchen, exulting in my freedom. Cold water drips down my wrist, and I smile. I passed their trial, and I recognize that the well and the spell have given this water other-worldly powers, and now it is mine.

I find myself in front of the grand staircase, but this time I am not propelled by the compulsion of the witches but the compulsion of my heart. I debate what to do next, the dribbling water braced on one hip, flickering my flashlight up and down the stairs. The rest of my water might leak out before I reach the children, and besides, in the fairy tales blood must atone for blood. Water will not be enough to revive them.

But the house will listen to me. I dash water from one banister all the way to the other.

> *"Stairs, obey my will and drink your fill!*
> *Test the heart of anyone who passes.*
> *Let none set foot who wishes ill.*
> *Protect my little lads and lasses. "*

I feel the settling in the house as it absorbs its new purpose. That should do it.

The clock strikes two. I can smell the first whiffs of cake, and it is more sweet than any pastry I have ever made. Nothing at all like frying up blood pudding. There is cackling in the living room, and I run into the courtyard.

I lean on the well, the stone rough on my palms. "How do I send the Horned Women away?"

The answer comes again. "Go to the north angle of the house, to the very top of the tower. Cry into the wind three times, and say 'the mountain of the Fenian women and all the sky over it is all on fire.'"

The Fianna are the ancient warrior bands who follow Fionn mac Cumhaill, and the Fenians can refer to them or—more often nowadays—the Irish Republican Brotherhood who fought for independence in the early twentieth century. The Fenian women could be either, I suppose. I trust the well and I trust myself.

Now that I know what to do, I am filled with urgent panic. I race to the other side of the courtyard, hoping that the tower stairs have reverted to the same period as the well, when they were solid and functional. But no, they are just like the workmen left them; blockaded by plywood and 2x4's, and my flashlight shows pebbles and stones littering the stairs. There's probably bats, or badgers.

I never wanted to go up there. But that makes me think of the children, the light in their eyes when they begged me to let them explore. For once, all united.

I pull at the first board, but it holds fast. I yank harder before remembering this is ridiculous. I must use my head.

I drag over a planter to climb on, but when I try to upend it the lemon tree fights back, stabbing my face with leathery branches and the block of soil stuck to the terracotta. Finally I get it out, my skirt now muddy and my hands smarting. Standing on the planter, I can just grip the top of the board and use the 2x4's to step on. I stick the flashlight in my mouth, although it tastes acrid and is probably all over germs. I scrabble and pull, my palms growing raw from grabbing at the unfinished plywood. I pause at the top, a board cutting into my stomach and ribcage, to check the other side with my flashlight. There are tumbled stones which I can use to scramble down, which is easier as long as I don't think about more of those stones falling on me. I aim, swing my legs over, and let go. It scrapes my thigh so painfully that I have to stop for a moment, gasping.

The smell of the cake is everywhere now. The walls are tight on either side of the tight spiral staircase, hemming me in, spider webs glob onto my face and something larger might jump out any minute. I find a stick and wave it in front of me. My pulse is pounding to hurry, run, quickly, but I force myself to climb carefully, shining my light back and forth to check for debris. If I slip and fall or get attacked by a badger, then I will not be able to fulfill my instructions, protect the household, and revive my children.

The door at the top of the tower is half-broken, but with all my strength I can shove it just enough to squeeze through. The wind catches my damp skirt and tangled hair, carrying such a scent of freedom that it makes me laugh out loud. The forest spreads out below me, the quarter-moon flits through gossamer clouds. Here I am! Even the smell of the cake cannot reach me here.

I cry out three times, half in fear for my children and half in anticipation. Clutching the stone balustrade, my hair flapping around my face, I shout the words that I learned from the well.

> *"The mountain of the Fenian women and all the sky over it is all on fire!"*

The Fianna come from the north beyond the moon, calling and laughing to each other on the wind. They fly on broomsticks and ravens and by their own sheer will; in the distance, in the distance, and then swooshing past my tower. I think they are both kinds of Fenians, although it is hard to see. They are screeching war cries in Irish and English, waving shillelaghs and hoes but also pistols and sewing shears.

They descend on the Great Hall, flying at the windows and door and vanishing instantly. I circle the tower to watch, but the walls stay solid and I can only guess what occurs within. I assume they are battling the horned women, and I am delighted. They make a great deal of noise.

After some time (three minutes? thirty?), the front door opens and twelve figures rush out, their line as neat and precise as ever. Then, a dozen blurry figures fly out of where the clerestory windows ought to be. Anxiety breaks through my exultation, as I imagine presenting Roy with the bill for every window in the Great Hall. He might call his lawyers in, for that, and I don't ever want to see a lawyer again, but how can we get through the winter with all the windows broken?

Come to think of it, I didn't hear the sound of shattering glass. Maybe they passed through like shadows.

Come to think of it, if I can wake the children and keep the Horned Women away, then I should be grateful for anything else. I should be, but lawyers are scary.

All is silent.

I can't stop now.

I make my way slowly down the staircase, each step shuddering into my knees and hips. I am so tired, and the stone is so unforgiving. Finally, moonlight in front of me—the delicious smell of the cake assaults me. The kitchen window is straight across from me, and I can see it on the counter.

But first, the plywood barrier. I groan. This time, with the witches gone, there is no adrenaline to help me reach higher or pull harder, just the dull awareness that I cannot stay back here all night. The children need me, their heartbeats slow and faint. My feet keep slipping when I try to climb the boulders. I grab for the top of the plywood and it hurts so badly, rubbing all the raw places. I haul myself up and can't help but cry. The plywood juts into my stomach, rips my legs. It all hurts, it is not fair; my anger has drained away and I am nothing but pain and exhaustion. Plan, Maura. I've got to land on the planter, not hit the paving stones and smash like an egg.

I catch it, landing hard with my balance wrong. I jump off the planter before I can fall, twist one ankle and tumble into the lemon tree.

Okay. That's done. Okay.

I limp back to the well, rubbing my fleece sleeves across my face. I sink onto the rim of the well, one arm around the post, the other fingers dangling. The cool water feels good on my hands, and I take a drink and splash my face. There. I am better. I must be better. Mothers do not have the option to give up.

"You have only one question remaining." The well startles me by speaking first. "Ask wisely, Maura."

The clock strikes three.

An owl hoots in the woods; a truck passes on the distant highway; I feel the heartbeats of the children sleeping in their beds. Other than the insidious smell of too-sweet cake, it is a normal night. I have time to sort through all the stories that I know and choose the right question.

"How do I protect this house so the Horned Women cannot return?" I finally ask.

"Ah, Maura, that is what you need to know. Listen carefully. Sprinkle your child's foot-water on the threshold outside the front door. Drop the crossbeam of the door into its jambs, and tie it in place with four threads from your four children's mending. And break apart the cake that the witches have baked, and place a bit in the mouth of each child who cannot wake—but do not eat even one crumb yourself, Maura."

"Thank you, oh, thank you! I shall do as you bid. Thank you." I bend and kiss the stone, then hurry towards the house, half-forgetting my scratches and aches. None of that will be difficult! I have made the magic and now I just need to tie it together, and we will all be safe. Safe!

I limp up the grand staircase, already planning what I will make for breakfast. I will call the children in sick from school; after all, they have lost a lot of blood. Waffles, I think. With thick Irish bacon and whipped cream and imported Vermont maple syrup.

Foot-water is from a time when children went barefoot and washing feet was a ritual. But Oliver, who tore his school uniform sliding down hills, does not disappoint. Under the covers, his feet are nice and grimy. I keep a bowl under the bathroom sink in case of vomit, and fill it with warm water. The plumbing in this wing is still working fine. I wash Oliver's feet—he does not stir, but the water goes a satisfying gray. I march downstairs and splatter it on the threshold, saying a rhyme for good measure. First step done!

The living room is an absolute disaster. Lamps are broken, spinning wheels cracked apart, picture frames splintered and shards of glass sparkling across the hearth. My sewing basket is knocked into a corner, tangled up in the mending. I find a working lamp. It takes a little while, but I sort out my needles and the threads I have used tonight. Four threads: girls primary uniform blue, boys primary uniform brown, gold for the bee and blue for the water.

It is satisfying to drop the crossbeam into the jambs, even though it stings my hands. My cold, scraped fingers stumble, but I am good with thread and I manage to get them tied. I put my hands on my hips, admiring my handiwork. I love that those delicate threads can hold the oak crossbeam in place, so it cannot leap to the witches' call. Two steps done!

The clock strikes four.

Now, just for the cake. And my children will wake! I long to kiss each one, even the big kids. I push open the kitchen door. The smell hits me and my stomach growls.

It's going to be delicious, but not for me. The nightlight in the corner is enough; I just want to get through this quickly. I place the cooling rack on the counter, put one hand on top, and flip the pan over.

And I find my hand almost at my mouth, clutching a fistful of cake.

"Maura! Stop!" I laugh, almost in surprise. I might be hungry—okay, starving—but the cake isn't for me.

I break the cake to put pieces in the pan, but I want to eat a chunk. I drop it, but raise my palm to lick it.

No.

I wipe my hands down my skirt, more desperately now. What is wrong with me? I lean forward, inhaling that blissful smell—and almost dip onto the counter and grab cake right in my mouth.

No!

I back away, clutching a kitchen chair to ground myself. This is ridiculous! Just break the cake into pieces. One into the mouth of each child. It will wake them from this strange, marble sleep, which is what I want most in the world. All of that love pounding through my veins, and the answer is right here. It's easy!

Except what I want most in the world is to eat that cake.

I am a strong woman. A smart woman. I can do this. Just bring it upstairs to my children.

Three times, I cross the kitchen and start to break the cake. Three times, my hands and mouth and arms disobey, trying to eat eat eat just one bite just one.

Cake in my hand—I cast it to the floor. Slap my own cheek. I pick up the cake with my left hand, a kitchen spoon poised in my right so I can whack my hand if it tries to feed me.

Want—I whack it.

Bring the cake towards my mouth.

Whack. This time I cry out.

My left hand is throbbing, but still pulled towards my mouth.

Whack, whack, whack. I am sobbing now, pain cutting through my fear and frustration.

I drop the cake and retreat behind the table, as though the flimsy thing can hold back the raging beast inside of me. I want that cake I want that cake. I drag the table and chair towards me, blocking myself into the corner, clutch the windowsill behind me, my left hand barely able to grip. My hair is flinging in my face like One-Horn's, I am sobbing and do not dare let go of the windowsill to wipe my snot away. My sweaty fingers slip free and I launch myself onto the table, which shudders under my weight. I need to get to that cake! I start crawling forward, the table swinging like a rowboat. Either to feed it to my children or to myself, I must have it!

The overhead light floods the room, white and yellow.

"What's going on in here?" Kaylee says. "It's been really loud tonight."

Oh yeah. Kaylee is not turned to marble sleep, because the Horned Women never touched her. I slide off the table onto a chair, trying to pull myself under control.

Kaylee's eyes are wide with fear, and she clutches her bathrobe tight. Her gaze swings to the counter, and she recoils. "What is that mess? And it smells disgusting! And don't say I'm yucking someone else's yum, because no one could like that smell! It's like dead skunk!"

"It smells...disgusting?" I can barely breathe through the ambrosia that assaults my nostrils. I am hungry and my hands are stinging and my ankle is throbbing and my thighs are frozen and chafed and splintered under my torn wet skirt. I just want that cake, but I have to think.

Kaylee doesn't even want the cake, which means that this yearning is for me, specifically. I cannot complete this story by myself.

The crone, the mother and...the maiden.

"Kaylee," I say, "I need your help."

I expect her to cringe, but instead she stands a little taller. "You need me? Can I do something? It's like...really there's a problem in here."

"It's really a problem," I agree. I feel a little more like myself now that I'm talking to Kaylee.

"Did you see the living room?"

"I did. We can sweep in the morning. But right now...Kaylee, I need you to take this cake upstairs. Your brothers and sisters are all..."

"Enchanted?" Kaylee offers.

"How did you know?"

"I looked for you in your bedroom, first. Oona and Oliver are just, like, laying there. They look weird. And there's dark stuff on the covers." Now Kaylee cringes a little, but just a little.

"Yes. One bite of this cake will restore them, and Aiden too. But listen, Kaylee—take the whole thing. Every single crumb. Don't leave any of it here."

"You trust me to do that?"

Motherhood is coming back to me, and I manage a reassuring smile. "You are the only one who can do it. I know you can, Kaylee."

"I'd better get some water." Kaylee pulls the wash-up tub down from the shelf—where did that come from?—and hurries to the well and back. She leaves the door open, and the fresh air clears my mind a little.

I clutch the table while Kaylee does a meticulous job of cleaning up the mess I have made, the counter and the floor and even wiping off the cooling rack so not a smudge is left.

"What do I do with the rest?" she asks, rinsing her rag. "What doesn't fit in their mouths."

"Flush it down the toilet," I say. It will meld with the castle's water and drain into our septic field, one with the land. The well can manage the evil cake.

"All right." She puts a paper towel over the cake pan to hold all the pieces in. "I'll be right back. Okay? Okay! Here I go!"

"There you go." I manage another smile. "You can do it."

Kaylee doesn't like the dark even in her own bedroom, she doesn't like the sound of the rain dripping from the eaves, and she refuses to light the fire because she's afraid she'll get burned.

But she must be brave, just the way she has been brave enough to stay this whole long month in a world that feels hostile at every turn.

Kaylee leaves the kitchen.

I draw a breath.

And another.

And something occurs to me. Kaylee can feed the three children, wake them all, finish the enchantment so the witches cannot return, and there still will be cake left over! There's no need to flush it down the toilet. I can have a bite. That's reasonable. I will make sure they are all awoken and safe. After the children have had their share, I can have a little. That is what mothers do; have the last sweet nibbles when their children are done. That is not selfish.

I rise from the table, wobbling a little on my bad ankle, and head for the grand staircase. Kaylee has turned on the lamp at the top of the hallway. "Wait, Kaylee!" I put my hand on the newel post and search for her upright figure. "Just a minute! Don't flush it away! Wait!"

It hasn't been long, so she can't be done yet. I step up the stairs, leaning on the balustrade to support my bad ankle—

And fall down again. Well, that was stupid.

I push myself painfully to my feet and start up the stairs again.

And fall.

How ridiculous! And I'm starting to get mad. I just need to get up and find Kaylee! I just want a bite of that cake!

I fall.

I hear Oliver, the sort of mumbled exclamation he often has in his sleep. His natural sleep, because he's had the cake, and all the children will get their share, I just want the bit that is leftover. That is not selfish!

"Let me have the leftovers!" I call, to Kaylee and the entire house. "Just save one bite for me!"

I try to step over the first stair, but fall again. I try on my hands and knees, but it is like climbing ice. I cannot make any headway; I just slide to the floor again. Everything hurts, but I am determined! I have done everything tonight, I must do this last thing! I try to pull myself up with the banister, but I collapse back down; I clutch and jump and flail. My knees are bruised and I am sobbing and I am leaving smears of blood with every grab. I don't understand, I am forgetting something, I don't know, but I must get up to my children, I must have that cake!

I wail her name, "Kayyyy-leeee!"

No one answers.

My head drops to the stairs, aching and throbbing. They are just normal stairs. I go up them every day. I will try one more time.

Smack, bang—I avalanche to the floor. The cake and my children, I must—

Above me, I hear the whoosh of a pull chain toilet, and everything is over.

I don't care about getting up the stairs.

I don't want to eat.

Everything hurts.

I curl into myself, cuddling my aching hand against my chest. I am cold, it is dark, and I cry. Silently. I have failed.

"Maura? They're sleeping now, the normal way. Maura!"

Footsteps on the stairs, poom-poom-poom-poom.

"Watch out for the—" I do not know what to say. I do not know why the stairs keep throwing me down, but Kaylee does not trip.

"Oh my god."

I hear the sob in her voice, and I am aching with guilt. It is too much, she is too young. I have failed.

There's a drag and a clunk and a click, and a lamp turns on over us. That's what Kaylee thinks of first, turning on the lights, and right now it's a darn good idea. I open my eyes and try to push myself up.

"Maura, oh my god! You're gonna be okay. I'm sorry. I'm sorry, Maura." Her hands on my shoulder, arm around my waist. She scoots us both, her lithe body pressed against mine. "Come here. I got you a blanket. It's one you made, it's really soft, I'm sorry, but I stole it for my room. Here you go...Mom."

She wraps us both in the blanket and we scoot against the wall. She drops her head onto my shoulder and I lean my cheek against her hair, both of us sagging and holding up the other. She clutches the quilt around us with one hand, and holds my hand with the other. I adjust the blanket so it covers our feet. We are all tucked away.

"It's okay, sweetie," I say.

"It's okay," she tells me.

We hold hands, tight. Nothing is okay.

The clock strikes five, and I hear a sound in the distance. It is a call of rage and vengeance.

We both tense.

"Open, open!" screams the voice, and eleven others echo the cry. "Open, feet-water!"

"I cannot," comes a reply, child-like and ghostly. "I am scattered on the ground, and my path is down to the Lough."

Kaylee shivers. I hold her tight.

"Open! Open, wood and trees and beam!" they scream.

"I cannot." This voice is deep and mournful. "The beam is fixed in the jambs, and my power is tangled in the threads."

"Aha, but we will have you yet! Open, open, cake that we have made and mingled with blood! You cannot refuse us entry, for the blood belongs in this house!"

"I cannot." This wailing, aching sob comes from all around us, shaking the stones beneath our bottoms. "For I am broken and bruised, and on the lips of the sleeping children."

"Ah! Ah! Ah!" The Horned Women scream and pound the walls, but I can feel that the stone does not give way. "We must retrieve our spindles and looms tonight, or we have lost our circle forever! Forevvvv-errrrr!!"

Kaylee and I bury our heads and hold each other fast as they pound and scream, scream and pound. Dawn comes late this time of year, but when it chases them away they will be gone. We will burn every scrap of spindle and loom, carding brush and knitting needle.

Kaylee shakes with quiet little—not even sobs, like that little sniff, that little chin quiver when her pudding didn't come out. I've learned to guard my heart, and Kaylee has learned to guard her feelings, and tonight all our guards are broken.

"Is it enough?" she whispers.

"The walls are strong. The door is closed." I squeeze her. "You did a good job."

"Really?"

"Forever! Forever!" the Horned Women cry. "Open, open!"

"I cannot." The deep voice.

"Really good," I tell Kaylee. "You were perfect."

And I realize what was good—her heart. I put the sanctified water on the stairs and asked them to test the hearts of those who pass, and they let Kaylee by but kept me on the floor.

What was in my heart? If I had gotten that cake, what would I have done to my little lads and lasses?

I shiver and Kaylee pulls the blanket tighter. The Horned Women scream and sob.

A few hours ago, I couldn't wait to sit down. Here I am, and I am definitely sitting, but this is not what I had in mind at all. I snug Kaylee close and hum to block out the noise. She murmurs words along with my tune, and I realize it's "Hallelujah."

The clock strikes six and all goes quiet.

We lift our heads, turn to look out a window. The sky is not bright, but the darkness has grown pale.

"What happened?" Kaylee asks.

I tell her the whole story. I leave nothing out.

"I don't think that cake was good for you," Kaylee says solemnly.

I can't help it, I start to laugh. And giggle and chortle and laugh some more. "I don't think it was," I agree, and Kaylee laughs with me, our breath warming us both.

"Look what I found when I was breaking it apart." She twists to reach into the pocket of her robe. "I washed them in the sink so there's no crumbs, but I didn't put them away so I wouldn't give one to the kids by accident. I forgot about them."

She opens her palm, and I shine my flashlight right at it. It is filled with little shiny pale curves, like toothpicks or puppy teeth, with a tiny ridged spiral.

"They're horns," she says. "Baby horns."

We count. There are thirteen.

"That would be for me," I say. I am horrified, but it finally makes sense. "It was a trap for me." I was not crazy or evil. "If I had eaten the cake, I would have become Thirteen-Horn."

"Don't touch." She closes her hand.

"They aren't calling to me now. It was just the cake."

"Okay, but still. I'm not taking any chances." She shoves them back in her pocket. "I'll bury them in the garden as soon as it's light. No wait. I'm not telling you where they're buried."

"Don't tell me, but I think I'm safe." I lean my head back against hers, feeling her relax into me.

"But we almost lost you." She sounds little and young, like she is. "If we didn't have you, that would—that would suck. It would suck elephant balls!"

I don't want to think about what Thirteen-Horn would have done to the children; it didn't happen. I'm still me, thank heavens. "I'll still be around, to make you scalloped potatoes and decorate for Christmas and—and love you every day." I swallow hard. I said the big word. I meant it.

It feels good, loving Kaylee.

"You remembered that I like scalloped potatoes," she says, in awe.

I'm worried that she's frightened of being left alone, and I'm not really essential. "But of course, if anything happened to me, you could always go back to your mother. Roy would take the little ones. Even without me, you guys are—"

"Now that," Kaylee interrupts, "that would suck dinosaur balls. Brontosaurus balls!"

I laugh again, and put both arms around her and she buries her face in my neck and laughs and cries and we hold each other tight. Maiden and mother and crone, and we have defeated the crones and kept our family safe. The edge of dawn glimmers at the top of the window.

"Hey," Aiden calls from the landing, mid-stairs. "For some reason, I couldn't sleep. Anyone want some tea?"

We do. Oh, how we want some tea.

"Will you make it, please?" Kaylee says, perfectly polite.

"Sure." Aiden ruffles his hair and yawns. "I just need to fetch the water."

Just like it is an ordinary morning. A new day, in my beloved ruined castle with my beloved children.

All four of them.

"Thank you," I answer. I have a suspicion that the well is going to behave for Aiden.

As for me, we're going to burn the looms and spinning wheels, and then just use a push broom to shove all the other debris out of the way. I'm going to ignore it. We can spend the day upstairs; my bedroom is big enough for all five of us, and Aiden can bring in his computer so we can watch a movie. Disney's fine.

We can deal with the Great Hall tomorrow. I'll send a bill to Roy for any damage, and if he makes a squeak I will stare him in the eye and remind him that I'm raising an awful lot of his children.

And then, I'm going to buy a new microwave. I don't mind dealing with jam on faces and algebra homework, but I draw the line at drinking lukewarm tea.

Besides, Kaylee can make a damn fine microwave pudding. I have full confidence in her.

The White Deer of Kildare

Raindrops slide down the windscreen of the Peugeot, and condensation creeps up the windows as we let the minutes creep by. We got to the Cork airport early, but Aiden and Kaylee haven't changed their minds. No way, no how are they getting on that plane back to America.

Aiden lifts his phone and snaps a picture of the distinctive swoop of the departures building, then turns and gets me in the frame. Ca-tip. Ca-tip. He hunches and his thumbs fly over the screen.

"Okay," Aiden says. "Done. It's official now."

He's trying to prove that I did my best to drop them off, but I know it won't be enough. The teens' biological parents are both going to blame me for violating the custody agreement.

Within seconds, my phone buzzes against my leg. In the back seat, Kaylee's pings, then dings, then chirps. Aiden, predictably, switched his to silent mode before unleashing the storm of recriminations. I should have done the same. I close my eyes and lean my head against the cold window. Buzz, buzz, chirp, ding.

"Are you sure you won't get out..." My voice can't turn this into a question.

"Have we missed the plane yet?" Kaylee demands.

"No," Aiden and I say together.

We sit without talking. More pings.

Amber: Please.

Please please please please please.

One mother to another. Please.

In my heart of hearts, I sympathize with Amber. I'd want to see my children for Christmas, too. I'd already be devastated if they chose a custody agreement with their former stepmother rather than with me. Then add losing Christmas together? I'd be dying. I feel so badly for Amber, but it's not like I can force two teens to board an international flight.

"Kaylee, are you sure?" I twist to look at the 13-year-old in the back seat. "It's just a few days. Your mother really wants to see you."

Kaylee leans forward, curtains of blond hair meeting to hide her face.

"You can come right back to Kilkenny," I say. "We can wait to celebrate Christmas until you get back. Don't you want to see your mother?"

"You're stupid!" Kaylee rears forward, flailing a hand against my seat. I wince.

"Stupid stupid stupid!" she shouts.

"Enough!" My voice is sharp and jagged.

She is breathing heavily, but I don't look back. I'm barely holding my composure. Another text buzzes, and I'm not surprised to see my ex-husband's name.

I never tried to get custody of Roy's older kids. I just wanted mine. The two we made together; the children I've held every day of their lives. I barely know Aiden and Kaylee, but I'm doing my best for them.

Kaylee makes a little sniffling gasp.

"It's okay," Aiden says. He twists back towards his sister, pats her knee. "It's okay. She just has to say it, remember? Maura has to show the grownups she's doing her part. That's why I sent the picture. She won't make you go."

"She will!"

I stare at the raindrops rolling down the window. This conversation isn't for me.

Kaylee sucks in a sob. "She just wants her own kids for Christmas, you know she does. She doesn't want either of us. She probably won't even let us in the house again."

Aiden sighs. "Kay-bear, Maura would let anyone come for Christmas. She'd invite her worst enemy if they were at the door."

"But don't you want to see your own mother?" I can't help it.

"I like the decorations better at the castle!" Kaylee shouts. "I spent all month clearing the dining room! I want to stay!"

"Okay." This is as much as I've gotten out of her. I know it's not the whole story, but I can't do any more.

Kaylee's phone pings a series of different tones. She says a word that I do not officially allow her to say, and I hear the little song that means she's shutting off her phone. I glance at the rearview mirror as she tosses it into the back of the car, bumping off their suitcases and clattering down the metal frame of the car. When she meets my eyes in the mirror, her face is flushed and her lower lip stuck out.

I bet it felt good to do that, but I have to deal with the adult stuff here. I swipe open my messages. I don't owe anything to Amber, her lawyer, her brother, or the kids' psychologist—all of whom are texting me—but I do need to answer Roy if I want to keep custody of my children.

> Roy: At the airport!
> Good job, Maura. I know Kaylee was being difficult.
> None of your location trackers have moved.
> Did Aiden leave his phone in the car?

Why is he showing in the parking lot?

You're all showing in the parking lot. Maura! What's going on?

The next few are mostly that word that I don't officially let Kaylee say, interspersed with my name. His aggression makes me frightened and shaky, and I close my eyes, visualizing the physical distance between us... an entire ocean and continent. He can't get me here. If he gets too mean, I'll be like Kaylee and turn the phone off.

Please be respectful, I type.

There, I'm standing up for myself. Roy can't see my wet eyes or the way I'm biting my lower lip.

Roy: Sorry.

I take a breath.

Aiden passes a Kleenex without looking at me. Kaylee shuffles her feet and sighs.

Roy: I know Kaylee can be a handful. Sorry babe.

Oh for—! I am not his babe. He has a newborn with another woman. And I don't know how to reply without making it sound like I'm agreeing to blame Kaylee for everything. Don't get me wrong, I'm totally frustrated with Kaylee. She's been sulking and stomping all week, and I've tried and tried to have a rational discussion about this but she just says that I don't understand, and I argue I can't understand if she doesn't explain anything to me, and I swear I have kept my voice calm and level. Every. Single. Time.

Roy: Listen, this is putting me in a pretty bad place.

Oh, you don't say? Poor Roy. Maybe you should have thought about this before going through three wives in a decade.

> Roy: So, could you just... Like pick up Kaylee and put her on the plane? Aiden will follow. You're bigger than Kaylee. You could get her out of the car.

My mixed feelings incinerate in a flash of rage.

> Me: I will not! I do not use physical force on children, even when they're toddlers!

> Roy: Aw, that's not true, babe.

> Me: It is!

> Roy: Oh yeah? I remember back when Oona was screaming herself sick, and you'd hold her poor little hips and force her seatbelt on her. More than once!

Is he seriously correlating putting a seatbelt on a one-year-old with dragging a thirteen-year-old through an entire international airport, and then what? Physically holding her on a plane until it takes off? I stare at my phone, seething.

> Roy: Maura?

The word wiggles and sparkles. He's tagging me in the conversation right in front of my face.

> Me: I'm sorry. But no, I can't force them out of the car.

Roy is going to keep showering me with texts until I don't know which way is up. I never figured out the right way to argue with Roy. He's going to start back in on the custody agreement, but my understanding of having custody is that I put the kids' needs first. And they need me.

I put the key in the ignition and glance in the rearview mirror. "I've got to get home before the little ones get home from school."

"Are you leaving me? Just leaving me at the airport here?" Kaylee's voice is panicked, breath fast, eyes wide. She clutches her seatbelt, as though someone is actually coming to drag her out of the car like a recalcitrant toddler.

Oh god, what have the adults in her life done to this poor child?

I switch off the engine and twist around.

Aiden puts his hand on his sister's knee. "Um, Kay-bear? We're both in the car. We're together."

We're all leaning into the middle of the Peugeot, and I can smell Kaylee's coconut hair gel and Aiden's nervous sweat.

"Have we missed the plane yet?" Kaylee turns to the window.

There's a hum and we all turn to watch a jet take off, our eyes tracking it into the air. That's not the one, but they're supposed to be at the gate by now. Even if they ran, even if they got special treatment, they couldn't make it through all the checkpoints before boarding.

"I've got to be there when the little kids get home," I repeat.

"Then we'd better go," Kaylee says.

I toss my phone to Aiden, press the clutch, and turn the key in the ignition.

Aiden turns it around in his hands, looking for the button to power down, and I'm sure there are more texts from Roy and Amber visible on my lock screen.

I wonder if he misses his mother.

***

Flustered by everything, I make a couple wrong turns driving out of Cork. With our phones all shut down and all the maps with them, I can't make sense of the streets. Roy's voice echoes in my head, You never did have any sense of direction. You're not practical, Maura. I yank the Peugeot towards an exit but change my mind—too late—the driver behind me slams on the brakes and then peels out around me, narrowly avoiding an accident. Heart pounding, I lurch down what is almost certainly the wrong road, almost stalling before I remember to downshift. Third, then fourth. Accelerate. Take a breath.

Roy is right. I can sew and cook and tell stories, but I'm no good at anything practical. Look, I can't even get them on an airplane.

"Uh, Mum?" Aiden rustles next to me. "I think you can take that turn. Up ahead, by the church? Yeah, that'll get us around."

I'm not his mum, but the word is starting to sound right to me. I focus on traffic, shifting at the right times, and Aiden tells me which lane and which turn, until we make it back onto the little county roads we both recognize. I breathe a sigh of relief and dare to check the dashboard clock.

Dang. School's already out, so I've got to beat the carpool home. I press the pedal and take the corners at Irish speed. Luckily the rain is tapering off.

Our castle is nearly an hour inland from Cork, along the twisty roads and rambling farmland between County Kilkenny and County Tipperary. When I was a little girl dreaming of living in a castle, I imagined being perched on a misty mountain or the surf crashing below rugged cliffs. When I was 31 and my husband left to live with his girlfriend, I couldn't sleep and kept browsing eclectic real estate listings and imagining living somewhere, anywhere, that I didn't have to look at him anymore. My lawyer kept saying what do you want, you're in a position to ask for things, and one night at three am I found a castle on Savills. It had a working roof and kitchen and was in a country that spoke English. I want that, I said.

It turns out that you cut across the corner of a cow pasture to get to my castle. Hardly the romantic setting I imagined, but it belongs to me and I love it fiercely. And on the upside, I don't have to worry about little kids falling off a cliff.

I take the turn from the south at the same time as the carpool hurtles around the curve from the north. We bounce down the gravel road, the minivan behind me, and through the gap in the looming whitethorn hedge. In the early Saxon period, this was an entire kingdom, but nowadays you can stand in the castle tower and see lorries driving by.

I pull to the side of the parking circle to give Claire O'Connelly room to turn around. I see the shadow of children's heads bouncing around in the van while Aiden and I get out and stretch. Kaylee slams her door and pops the trunk.

Mrs. O'Connelly comes around her van, smiling in her bland way. "Nice to have the holidays, innit? Kiddies all home for Christmas."

"Lovely." I smile on the outside, although Kaylee and Aiden are at the wrong home for Christmas and I can't stop worrying about it. Roy's probably called the lawyers by now, but I can't have him trying to take Oona and Oliver. I'll have to figure something out.

Kaylee throws a backpack on the wet gravel. "I decorated the Long Gallery." Scowling, she points a finger to the wall above our heads.

Mrs. O'Connelly and I turn obediently to look; Kaylee has that effect on people.

"Well then, that's lovely." Mrs. O'Connelly gives the van door an expert yank. "I brought Oliver's friend Oisín no problem, but text me first the next time you're going to need an extra seat, won't you?"

Did I schedule a playdate and forget about it? I apologize automatically.

"No worries." Mrs. O'Connelly smiles in her bland way. "It'll be great fun anyhow, Oliver having a friend to stay for the whole holidays."

Now wait. I am positive that I did not invite a child to come stay with us for two weeks.

Oliver jumps down with his gap-tooth smile and a diorama in one hand. "Hi, Mum!"

Another little boy follows, with an equally round face and equally wide smile. "Hi, Oliver's mum!"

They both roar like dinosaurs, throw their arms around me, and pretend to eat my jacket.

I'm a little stunned. I stare after them as they take off in a wild loop around the Peugeot and into the shrubbery, diorama waving. Aiden helps Oona with her papers and opens the castle door for her, but Kaylee is as shocked as I am, her mouth gaping as she watches the boys run.

"Now then, Maura"—Mrs. O'Connelly sidles closer to me, her brows lowering—"I know you Americans have all these problems with race, but this isn't the time or place. His name is Oisín, which is a nice Irish name, and he sounds just like we do. So he's a nice Irish boy and never you mind the color of his skin, you hear?"

"Of course not. Of course."

Kaylee meets my gaze, eyes round as cookies. We aren't shocked by the rich brown of Oisín's skin, we are shocked because he is buck naked and no one else seems to notice. We saw some strange women a few weeks ago, Kaylee and I, but that was in the middle of the night and inside the castle. Right now it's four in the afternoon and we're talking with a pragmatic mother with a van full of primary school kids. This is normal life, right here, right now.

"Oh, and I've got his dog too." Mrs. O'Connelly trundles around to the back of the van.

What the ever-loving—? This child I have never heard of has brought his dog?

"Wouldn't want to leave her in town now, would we." She opens the gate and pets something inside. "She a lovely girl now, innit? Traditional breed, the deerhound." She steps aside and snaps her fingers, and the animal leaps gracefully to the ground.

"Bye, puppy!" the children chorus from inside the van.

Kaylee and I exchange another look.

That is not a dog.

Right then. A custody argument with my ex was only the beginning, and this is not going to be a normal afternoon at all.

***

What happens with the custody arrangements, and who is the dog who is not a dog? Click here to read The White Deer of Kildare, and fall back into the Ireland of ancient myth with Maura. Can she make it home alive?

https://bf.christymatheson.com/exmh6b6hgx

About the Author

Characters you connect with. Adventure. Love. Family. And endings that are more than a sugar rush.

When Christy Matheson is not throwing ordinary characters into fairy tales, she is busy raising five children. (Very busy.) She writes character-driven historical fiction with and without fantasy elements, and her "fresh, smart, and totally charming" stories have won multiple awards.

Christy is also an embroidery artist, classically trained pianist, and sews all of her own clothes. She lives in Oregon, on a country property that fondly reminds her of a Regency estate (except with a swing set instead of faux Greek ruins), with her husband, five children, three Shelties, one bunny, and an improbable quantity of art supplies.

Please join Christy in conversation about books and determined women throughout history.

Join her newsletter to get free stories, art giveaways, & puppy pictures. https://sendfox.com/ChristyMatheson

And you can always find her at: ChristyMatheson.com